# How Many Seeds?

Written by Monica Halpern

Steck Vaughn

HOUGHTON MIFFLIN HARCOURT
Supplemental Publishers

www.SteckVaughn.com
800-531-5015

Most fruit has seeds inside.

How many seeds are in a peach?

 3

A peach has one seed.

How many seeds are in an apple?

An apple has a few seeds.

How many seeds are in a watermelon?

A watermelon has many seeds!